NICK JR.

DORA the EXPLORER

PHONICS
READING PROGRAM

Book 4
short u

Stuck in the Mud!

by Quinlan B. Lee

SCHOLASTIC INC.
New York   Toronto   London   Auckland   Sydney
Mexico City   New Delhi   Hong Kong   Buenos Aires

What a sunny day!
Boots and I love to run
and chase after butterflies.

Stop!
Do you see something
under that bush?
It is a Bugga Bugga baby.
But what is she doing
under those shrubs?

Uh-oh!
The little bug is stuck
in the mud.
Come on!
We must pull her out
and get her back home.

There's so much mud!
How can we get her
unstuck without getting
stuck in the muck, too?
Right!
Jump on the rocks.

Good jumping!
Now we're close enough.
Come on, Baby Bugga
Bugga.
We will help you up
and out of the mud.

We did it!
But now we must
take her home.
I wonder where
Bugga Bugga bugs live.

Bugga Bugga bugs
love flowers.
With some luck,
we can find her momma
in this bunch of flowers.

Yay! The baby bug is back
with her mother.